The Case Of The
SLAM DUNK MYSTERY™

Look for more great books in

series:

The Case Of The Great Elephant Escape™
The Case Of The Summer Camp Caper™
The Case Of The Surfing Secret™
The Case Of The Green Ghost™
The Case Of The Big Scare Mountain Mystery™

and coming soon
The Case Of The Rock Star's Secret ™

The Case Of The
SLAM DUNK MYSTERY™

by Cathy East Dubowski

HarperEntertainment
A Division of HarperCollins*Publishers*

A PARACHUTE PRESS BOOK

PARACHUTE PRESS

Parachute Publishing, L.L.C.
156 Fifth Avenue
New York, NY 10010

DUALSTAR PUBLICATIONS

Dualstar Publications
c/o Thorne and Company
A Professional Law Corporation
1801 Century Park East, Twelfth Floor
Los Angeles, CA 90067

HarperEntertainment

A Division of HarperCollins*Publishers*
10 East 53rd Street, New York, NY 10022–5299

For information, address HarperCollins Publishers Inc.
10 East 53rd Street, New York, NY 10022–5299

ISBN: 0-06-106588-9

HarperCollins®, ⬛®, and HarperEntertainment™ are trademarks of
HarperCollins Publishers Inc.

First printing: January 2000

Printed in the United States of America

Visit HarperEntertainment on the World Wide Web at
http://www.harpercollins.com

10 9 8 7 6 5 4 3 2 1

1

A NEW CASE?

"Lemons are sour,
Candy is sweet.
Mustang girls just
Can't be beat!
Go, Mustangs!"

My twin sister, Ashley, and I shouted the cheer with the rest of our basketball team. Our team is called the Mustangs. And we were cheering like crazy—because we were in the play-offs! All right!

I glanced around the empty gym. Soon it would be full of excited Mustang fans. I couldn't wait!

We have an awesome team. Our star player is Tara Ledbetter. Her older brothers taught her to play when she was three. She has a killer layup!

"Hey, shrimp," Shanaya Perry called to me with a grin. Shanaya is our tallest player. My head only comes up to her shoulder!

"Who are you calling a shrimp?" Kerry Collins asked as she jogged onto the court. Her curly brown hair bounced with each step. She gave Shanaya a gentle punch in the arm. Kerry is the shortest player—even shorter than me—but she's as good as Shanaya.

I smiled at the other players on our team—our best friend, Samantha Samuels, and Emily Bailey, Joanne Lundy, and Kristen Duffield.

Coach Kay tries to give everyone a chance to play, but Samantha, Emily, Joanne, and Kristen aren't our best players, so they don't play as often as everyone else. I think Kristen went out for the team only because her friend Joanne did. Her favorite part of the game is sitting on the bench and reading.

For the play-offs we have to play three games against the Tigers, from Glen Morgan Elementary School. Whoever wins gets to go on to the championships.

We had already won the first game. And I had a feeling we were going all the way!

"Okay, girls," said Coach Kay. "I want you to remember three things. Play fair. Remember that you're a team. And most of all—"

"Score the most points?" Ashley joked.

Coach Kay laughed. "That would be nice, too. But what I was going to say was—be sure to have a good time. That's what basketball is all about."

We all cheered again. Then Coach Kay glanced at her watch. "Time to get dressed, girls. I'll meet you back out here in five minutes for a pregame warm-up."

We headed for the locker room to put on our team jerseys. They were laid out in a pile on one of the benches. Emily Bailey's dad is our sponsor. He runs a laundry business. He bought us our team shirts—and he cleans them after each game for free.

I love my jersey. It has my name on the back in big black letters. I couldn't wait to put it on.

Except...I couldn't find it anywhere. I dug through the pile again. But it wasn't there.

"Hey! My jersey is missing!" I said.

Ashley was digging through the pile of jerseys, too. She looked up, frowning. "I don't see mine, either."

"Me either," Shanaya said. Then she

leaned down and picked up a jersey that had fallen on the floor. "Oh, here it is."

Ashley and I stood by as the other girls found their shirts and put them on. The bench was empty—no more shirts.

"Hey, mine is missing, too," Tara said.

"So is mine," Kerry added. "This is weird."

"I smell a mystery," Samantha said. Her freckled face split into a grin, and she dug an elbow into my ribs.

Everyone else laughed. But I didn't.

Ordinarily, I love mysteries. Ashley and I are detectives. We have our own agency, the Olsen and Olsen Mystery Agency.

But I didn't want a mystery right now. Not when the second game of the play-offs was about to start!

"We'd better get to work, Ashley," I said. "We have to solve the Mystery of the Missing Jerseys—and fast!"

2

THE MYSTERY OF THE MISSING JERSEYS

"**N**ow, let's think about this, Mary-Kate," Ashley said. "Just because something's missing doesn't make it a mystery. There could be lots of reasons the jerseys aren't here."

That's Ashley for you. She likes to be sure before she acts. I usually just jump right in.

"Okay," I said. "Got any ideas?"

Ashley glanced at Emily. "Maybe Emily's dad left some out by accident."

Hmmm. I never thought of that.

Emily looked embarrassed.

"Well, girls, ready to play?" Coach Kay asked as she came into the locker room.

"We can't!" Tara told her. "Someone stole our jerseys!"

"What?" Coach exclaimed.

"Uh, well, we don't know that for sure," Ashley said. "But four shirts are missing. Tara's, Kerry's, Mary-Kate's, and mine."

"Oh," Coach Kay said. "Well, I guess they didn't come back from the laundry."

Ashley looked at me and raised her eyebrows. I sighed.

Sometimes I wish *I* were as logical as Ashley.

Kerry sank down on a bench. "What will we do?"

"Will they have to miss the game?" Emily asked.

Coach Kay shook her head. "Don't worry. Fortunately, there's no rule that says you can't play in regular clothes."

"But I can't play without my lucky jersey!" Tara said. "I've worn it in every game this season."

Coach smiled. "Tara, your clothes don't have anything to do with your talent. You're a very good player! Now, don't worry. Let's just go out there and do our best!"

We all headed out onto the court.

The Tigers were already warming up. Their brand-new blue-and-yellow uniforms looked so cool. I felt weird wearing my faded Camp Wishing Well T-shirt. It seemed as if everyone in the whole gym was staring at us. I saw Jillian Shelton jab one of her teammates with her elbow and snicker.

Jillian Shelton is the Tigers' captain. She's a great player, but she can be pretty rough. In the first game, she ran into Joanne and knocked her down so hard, Joanne got a bloody nose. Jillian didn't even say she was sorry.

Jillian stared at my T-shirt and grinned. I know it shouldn't have mattered what she thought. But it did. I felt dopey. And I could tell Ashley, Tara, and Kerry did, too.

And when the game started, that's how we played—like dopes! We were terrible! We fouled. We dropped the ball. We went out-of-bounds.

Tara really played poorly. "It's because I don't have my lucky jersey," she whispered to me.

Jillian roared up the court with the ball. She began to line up a shot.

Ashley ran up to block her. I was right behind Ashley, so I saw exactly what happened next. Jillian lunged to one side—and shoved Ashley with her shoulder as hard as she could! On purpose!

Ashley crashed into me. We both fell. I bonked my head on the polished wood floor.

I heard the time-out whistle blow as

Ashley scrambled to her feet. She faced Jillian. "Why did you shove me?" Ashley demanded in a furious voice.

Jillian acted surprised. "What?" she said, playing innocent. But I saw her give Ashley a nasty grin.

Ashley glared at her for another second. Then she reached down to help me up. "Mary-Kate, are you all right?"

"I'm fine." I rubbed my head. It hurt a little—but not that badly. Coach Kay made me sit out for a while, anyway. Just to make sure I was okay.

I sat down on the bench next to Emily. Joanne, Kristen, and Samantha were there, too.

Emily jumped up. "Can I go in for Mary-Kate?" she begged Coach Kay.

"Maybe next time," Coach Kay said. Then she sent in Samantha to take my place.

"She never lets me play," Emily grumbled.

She kicked the cooler that held our water bottles. Then she plopped back down on the bench.

I watched the game on the edge of my seat. Tara dribbled toward our basket. But then—oh, no! Jillian swooped in and stole the ball!

The Tiger fans cheered as Jillian jumped up to shoot. Tara jumped to block the shot. But she didn't jump high enough.

SWISH! The ball sailed through the net. Three points for the Tigers! Jillian pumped her fists in the air.

"Coach should have put me in the game," Emily complained. She scuffed her brand-new basketball sneakers on the gym floor. "Tara let us down. I would have stopped Jillian cold!"

I shrugged. *Easy to say when you're sitting on the bench*, I thought.

We were in the last few minutes. Coach Kay asked for a time-out. She signaled

Samantha to come back to the bench.

Emily jumped up. "Put me in, Coach. Please? Tara's playing lousy. Give me a chance."

Oops. That was a big no-no. I saw Coach Kay purse her lips. She really didn't like it when a girl put another player down.

"Mary-Kate, you're back in," she called.

I glanced at Emily. *Sorry*, I mouthed, as I ran out onto the court.

But for the rest of the game, we Mustangs just couldn't seem to make it work. I missed a pass. Kerry blew a free throw.

The game was almost over. The Tigers were ahead by one point. *We can still win*, I thought as I ran down the court.

Tara had the ball—and I was open for an easy shot! "Tara!" I called out.

Tara passed me the ball.

I crouched down and sprang up to shoot.

I shot—

Thunk!

The ball bounced off the rim! I missed!

The referee blew the whistle.

The game was over. And we lost by one point!

I walked off the court very, very slowly. I didn't want to face my teammates. I didn't want to face the coach.

How could I have missed that shot? How?

Ashley put her arm around my shoulder. "Don't feel bad."

"Yeah," said Kerry. "It's not your fault."

Tara looked really disappointed. But she said, "We all miss shots sometimes."

Kristen and Joanne patted me on the shoulder.

Emily stared down at the floor. Then she jerked her head up and stared at me.

"How could you miss that basket?" she shouted.

I blinked in surprise.

"It was an easy shot!" she went on. "I *told* Coach to send me in. I wouldn't have missed. Then we would have won!" She shook her head. "Thanks for losing the game, Mary-Kate."

I felt as if someone had just punched me in the stomach. "I'm sorry," I murmured.

"Back off, Emily. It wasn't Mary-Kate's fault," Shanaya said.

A girl with a long blond braid came toward us from the bleachers. She looked sort of familiar—but I couldn't think of her name. Did she go to our school?

"Hey, guys," the girl said with a smile. "Sorry about the game. But, well, I guess that's how it goes." She was holding something in her arms. It looked like a pile of clothes. "I found these during the game."

She held up a basketball jersey. Across the back, in big black letters, was my name, MARY-KATE.

"My jersey!" I cried.

We checked out the other three. Sure enough, they belonged to Ashley, Tara, and Kerry.

"Where did you find these?" Ashley asked.

The girl shrugged. "They were stuffed up in the bleachers, behind my seat." She handed them over. "See you around," she said, and headed toward the exit.

"So how did our shirts wind up in the top bleachers?" I asked my sister.

Ashley's eyebrows drew together. "I don't know. Something strange is definitely going on here." Her frown deepened. "Maybe you were right, Mary-Kate. Maybe we do have a mystery to solve!"

SIGN OF TROUBLE

Ashley and I climbed the steps of the bleachers. We searched around the top row of seats. We were looking for clues. Anything that might tell us who stole our jerseys.

But we didn't find anything. Except a couple of gum wrappers, that is.

"Mom and Dad are waiting for us in the car," Ashley reminded me after a few minutes. "We'd better go before they start to wonder where we are."

"Okay," I said. "I just have one question. Are Olsen and Olsen on the case?"

"You bet!" Ashley said.

It was Sunday, two days after we lost the game. Ashley, Samantha, Emily, Tara, and I met at the school. Our friend Tim Park came along, too.

Our school has a big message board out front by the main entrance. It's where they put up signs like PTA MEETING TONIGHT or TUESDAY IS PICTURE DAY. Anything kids or parents might need to know.

We got permission to put up a message about the next basketball game. We thought it would cheer up the team after losing the last one.

Ashley and I parked our bikes and walked toward the message board. I took a box of black magnetic letters out of my backpack. The school secretary loaned them to us to put up our message.

"How about this?" I said. I placed letters on the board to spell out:

LET'S GO MUSTANGS!
YOU CAN DO IT!

"Hey, check out that girl!" Tim suddenly exclaimed. He pointed toward the basketball court at the far end of the schoolyard.

A girl in a gray hooded sweatshirt was shooting baskets. I squinted to see who it was. Her long blond braid bounced up and down as she played.

"It looks like that girl who found our jerseys," I said.

"I know her," Tim said. "That's Becky Davis. She just transferred to our school. She's in my class."

"She's good!" Samantha exclaimed.

"How come she's not on your team?" Tim wanted to know.

"Maybe she doesn't want to be on the

team," Emily suggested.

"Or maybe nobody asked her," Ashley said. "Come on. Let's go talk to her. She could blow Jillian out of the water." Her eyes narrowed. "You know, I bet Jillian had something to do with hiding our jerseys. That's just the kind of rotten person she is! Mary-Kate, we should check it out."

Whoa. Now Ashley was jumping to conclusions! I guess she was still angry about the way Jillian pushed her during the game.

"Wait," I said. "Let's finish up our sign first."

"What else does it need?" Emily asked.

Tara picked up some letters. "We should tell when the game is." She added:

NEXT GAME WILL BE FRIDAY NIGHT

"That looks great!" Ashley said.

I closed the box of letters and put them into my backpack. Then we all headed over to the basketball court.

But Becky was gone.

"Too bad—I wanted to go one-on-one with her," Tara said. "Oh, well. I brought a ball." She held up her bulging backpack and took out a basketball. "Anyone want to shoot a few hoops?"

We all took turns shooting foul shots for about half an hour. Then it was time to go home.

Ashley and I headed back to our bikes. "Look!" Ashley said. "Somebody's already checking out our sign." She stopped and pointed.

I squinted. There were two kids by the sign, but the sun was shining in my eyes and it was hard to see who they were.

One of them wore a gray hooded sweatshirt with the hood up over her head.

"Isn't that Becky Davis?" I asked.

"I'm not sure." Ashley's eyes suddenly widened. "But that other girl is definitely

Jillian Shelton—from the Tigers!"

"Huh?" I said. "What's she doing here?"

Ashley looked at me. "Come on. Let's go find out!"

She took off. I ran after her.

But before we could get close enough to talk to them, Jillian and the other girl spotted us. They turned around and ran off!

4

A Mean Trick

"**H**ey, stop!" Ashley shouted. But the two girls kept running.

We raced up to the sign. "Oh, no!" I groaned.

The letters in our message had been scrambled. Our cheerful words were gone. Now the note said:

MUSTANGS CAN'T WIN!

Ashley stared at the sign. "Those rats!"

she cried. Then she spun around and ran to the bike rack. "Come on! Let's get them!"

We hopped on our bikes and pedaled as fast as we could. But when we reached the corner, they were gone.

"I can't believe it!" Ashley exclaimed. "We lost them! Oh, I am so mad! Jillian Shelton should be kicked off her team. I'm going to report her to Coach Kay!"

"We can't," I said.

She frowned at me. "Why not?"

"Because we don't have proof that Jillian did this!" I patted my sister's arm. "I know how upset you are. I am, too. But we really do need proof before we can complain about it."

Ashley's shoulders sagged. "You're right."

"Can you believe this?" I laughed. "For the first time, *I'm* telling *you* to slow down until we get all the facts!"

Ashley laughed, too. Then we rode back

to school, fixed the sign, and biked home.

"There's something I want to know," I said as we rode. "What was Becky Davis doing with Jillian? How do they know each other?"

"We can't be sure that was Becky," Ashley pointed out. "We didn't get a good look at her. All we saw for sure was a gray sweatshirt."

We rolled to a stop in front of our house. I got off my bike. But Ashley didn't budge. "Come on," she said. She had a determined look on her face.

"Where are we going?" I asked.

"To Jillian's house," she told me. "Let's ask her what she was doing at our sign."

"But, Ashley—"

Ashley started to bike away.

"Ashley! Wait!" I called.

Ashley stopped. "What's wrong?" she asked.

"We can't go," I said.

"How come?" she asked.

"Because—we don't know where Jillian lives," I pointed out.

Ashley blushed. "Oh, yeah."

We went inside to look Jillian up in the phone book. She lived on Maple Avenue.

"That's not far from here," I said. "Let's go there now!"

We jumped on our bikes and rode over.

Jillian was in her driveway shooting baskets. We parked our bikes on the sidewalk and walked right up to her.

She looked at us suspiciously. "What do you want?" she asked.

I started to speak.

But Ashley blurted out, "We saw you switch the letters on our sign!"

Jillian didn't say anything. She just kept dribbling and shooting. She didn't even look at us.

"Well?" Ashley asked.

"You can't prove anything," Jillian said.

She made another shot. *Swish!*

Wow, I thought. *She's cool—even under pressure.*

"We saw you," I said.

"We're going to report you," Ashley said. "So you might as well tell the truth."

Jillian caught the ball and glared at Ashley. "Oh, yeah?" she said. "Well, my mom just happens to be the principal of Glen Morgan Elementary. So if you plan on accusing me of pulling pranks like that, you'd better have super proof. In fact, you'd better have it on videotape!"

I started to reply, but Jillian's mom came to the door. "Jillian," she called. "Phone for you. It's Becky Davis."

Jillian hurried inside. "So Becky does know Jillian!" I said. "That *had* to be Becky with Jillian messing up our sign."

"I guess so," Ashley said. "Hey, I just thought of something else. The jerseys! Becky was the one who found our team jerseys in the bleachers after the game."

"Whoa. Do you think maybe she found them because *she* hid them there in the first place?" I asked.

"Maybe," Ashley said.

"But why would Becky help Jillian?" I asked. "Why would she help the Tigers? That's no way to make friends at a new school."

"I don't know," Ashley said. "But we're going to find out!"

After dinner that night we cleared the table. Then we went on-line on our computer for a little while.

Ashley clicked the little picture of a mailbox to check our E-mail. We had a letter from our mom. It read:

"Do you girls have homework?"

We both groaned.

Suddenly some new mail popped up. *Chatty Patty*, it read.

I groaned again. *Chatty Patty* was an on-line newspaper written by our neighbor, Princess Patty.

Well, that's not her real name. That's just what Ashley and I call her. Her real name is Patty O'Leary. But she acts like a princess. Not the good kind. The spoiled kind!

Princess Patty just got a new computer. That's when she started writing *Chatty Patty* and sending it to everybody at school.

Ashley clicked on it, and the story opened.

We both read the headline:

SPORTS NEWS:

TEARS INSTEAD OF CHEERS

FOR MUSTANG GIRLS B-BALL

BY MISS PATTY O'LEARY

CHATTY PATTY SPORTS REPORTER

"*Chatty Patty* sports reporter?" I said,

laughing. "She's the *only* reporter on her newspaper."

Ashley and I kept reading.

Friday was a sad day for the Mustangs! Boo-hoo! :(The girls' basketball team lost their second play-off game to Glen Morgan Elementary School!

What's up, girls? We had a chance to win. All we had to do was make one more basket! But one of our players—and you know who you are—missed an easy shot. Maybe she might have more fun watching the game from the bench next time!

I slumped in my seat. That hurt!

"That's just plain mean," Ashley said.

"But Patty's right," I muttered.

"No, she isn't. None of us were playing very well," Ashley told me. "The missing jerseys threw us off. But if we concentrate better next time, I know we can win."

I love Ashley. She always knows how to cheer me up!

"Okay," I said. "But I still want to find proof that Becky and Jillian are the ones who took our jerseys."

"Right!" Ashley agreed. "We'll solve our case *and* win the play-offs. Because Olsen and Olsen are a team that can't be beat!"

5

HOOP SNOOPS

The next day at school everyone was talking about the latest edition of *Chatty Patty*.

"Never mind," Ashley whispered. "Just think about our case."

Our class had art every Monday morning with Ms. Lacy. We were making stained-glass window hangings out of sheets of colored plastic. I was making a fairy. I stuck the pieces together with glitter glue.

We sat at big tables. Ms. Lacy let us talk

as we worked, as long as we didn't get too loud.

Emily Bailey took a seat next to me. "I guess you saw the *Chatty Patty* story, huh?" she asked.

"Uh-huh," I said.

"It was mean," Emily said. She looked at the table. "Are you going to drop out, like she said?"

"No way!" I declared.

Across the table Shanaya shook her head. "Patty's just jealous because she didn't make the team."

"Girls…" Ms. Lacy smiled. "Not so loud." She put a finger to her lips.

Emily squeezed out some glitter glue. She was making a glittery basketball.

I lowered my voice. "Hey, does anybody know anything about that new girl, Becky Davis?"

Samantha shook her head. "Just that she's new."

"Does anybody know where she came from?" Ashley asked.

Shanaya thought a minute. "I think I heard somebody say she used to go to Glen Morgan."

Ashley and I stared at each other. That explained a lot!

"Yeah, I heard that, too," Emily said. "I heard she even played on their basketball team. The Tigers. Her mom came into my dad's store to set up an account. I heard her bragging about her daughter."

It was all starting to make sense now.

Becky was definitely the Tigers' spy!

Then I thought of something else.

If Jillian and Becky were really trying to mess up the Mustangs, they might try again. They might pull another prank.

We'd have to watch out!

Our next chance to talk about the case was on the playground at recess.

"Coach Kay keeps the gym locked before and after school," Ashley said. We were turning two jump ropes for double Dutch.

"That means Becky had to steal the jerseys during school hours," I said.

It was Emily's turn to jump. She dashed into the twirling ropes and began to jump quickly.

"Emily," Ashley asked her as we turned the ropes. "Remember when our jerseys disappeared?"

Emily kept jumping. "Sure."

"When did you bring them in from your dad's laundry?" I asked.

Emily turned toward me, still jumping. "I brought the clean jerseys to school with me that morning."

"Did you take them straight to the gym?" I asked.

Emily stepped on the rope and missed. "Rats!"

"Did you take the shirts straight to the gym?" I asked again. "Or did you do something else with them?"

Emily wrinkled up her nose, trying to remember. "Oh, yeah. I was late that morning," she said. "So I kept the shirts in our classroom. I dropped them off at Coach Kay's office right before silent reading."

Silent reading was right after lunch. About one o'clock.

"Thanks, Emily," I said.

Ashley and I passed the ropes to two other girls to turn. We went off and sat under a tree.

"What next?" I said.

Ashley slipped her notebook out of her pocket. The notebook and my mini tape recorder were presents from our great-grandma Olive. She's a detective, too. She's the one who first got us started solving mysteries.

Ashley made a note in her notebook.

"We need to find out where Becky was last Friday between one o'clock and the end of school."

"I doubt she'll tell us," I said.

"We need a witness," Ashley said. "Someone who saw her coming in or out of Coach Kay's office."

"Who might have seen Becky that day?" I thought out loud.

Ashley shrugged. "Anybody who's in her class."

We looked at each other. "Tim!" we said at the same time. Tim Park was in Becky's class!

At lunchtime Ashley had to go back to her locker for a book. I went looking for Tim. He was sitting in the lunchroom with some kids from his class. He was easy to spot because he's so tall and skinny, and because his hair is jet-black.

I told Tim that Ashley and I were working on a mystery, and I needed to ask him a few questions. "It's important," I added.

"Fire away!" he said.

"Where was your class at one o'clock on Friday?" I asked him.

Tim thought for a moment. "Art class," he said. "We're making clay animals. I'm making a hippopotamus!"

I nodded. "What time did you go to the art room?"

"One o'clock. On the dot," he added. "You know how Ms. Lacy likes everyone to be on time."

"Was Becky Davis there that day?" I asked.

"I guess so." Tim frowned and chewed a bite of his baloney sandwich. "No, wait!" he said. "I remember. She was late that day. She came running in out of breath. Ms. Lacy had a talk with her about being late."

"Why was she late?" I asked.

Tim shrugged. "I didn't hear that part."

It didn't matter. I knew why she was

late! She was hiding our basketball jerseys!

"Thanks, Tim," I said. I headed back to our table just as Ashley sat down.

"Guess what?" I said excitedly. "I found out an important clue." I unwrapped my turkey sandwich and took a bite. "Tim said Becky came in five minutes late to their one o'clock art class. That means she had time to steal the team jerseys."

Ashley wrote the new information in her notebook. "That's one step closer. But it still doesn't prove that Becky did it. If we told Coach Kay now, Becky could just say she had to go to the bathroom or something."

"Well, maybe we should ask her about it," I said. "It can't hurt to try."

I scanned the lunchroom until I spotted Becky. She sat by herself at an empty table. I guess she didn't know many people yet, being new.

We walked over to Becky. She looked

up. Her eyes widened at the sight of us.

"Hi," she said. She sounded nervous.

"Hi. I'm Mary-Kate, and this is my sister, Ashley," I said. "Listen, we saw you hanging out with Jillian Shelton on Sunday."

Becky's cheeks turned red. "No, I wasn't!"

"But we saw you," Ashley said. "Mary-Kate and I. You helped Jillian mess up our sign."

"No, I didn't!" Becky cried. A few kids turned to stare at her. Her cheeks turned even redder.

"Okay, I was there," she said in a quieter voice. "But I didn't do anything to the sign. I was trying to *stop* Jillian from ruining it."

"Then why did you run away?" I asked.

"I—I—," Becky stammered.

She sure was acting guilty!

"Never mind," I said to Becky. "Tell me this: How come you were late to art class last Friday?"

Becky stared at me. "Huh? What is this?"

she demanded. "Why are you asking me all these questions?"

"We know you used to play for the Tigers," Ashley said. "We think you've been helping Jillian to mess up the Mustangs so we'll lose the play-offs."

Becky jumped to her feet. "That's crazy!" she shouted. "I don't have to listen to you!"

She grabbed her books and stormed off. Ashley and I looked at each other.

"She's definitely guilty," I said. "But we still don't have proof."

"Right," Ashley said. "Time for serious action. Mary-Kate, we're going to stake out Becky's house!"

STAKEOUT!

*S*nap!

"Shhh!"

"Sorry!"

It was the same day, after school. We didn't have basketball practice. So Ashley and I were following Becky home. I had just stepped on a twig.

We kept near trees and shrubs that lined the sidewalk. We've had a lot of practice following people without getting caught. Detectives have to do it all the time.

But this was too easy. Becky never once looked back.

Nothing unusual happened on the way home. Becky walked all alone. She kicked a soda can down the sidewalk, then put it in a trash can. She stopped to pet a cat.

At last we reached her house. We hid across the street behind a big blue-and-red mailbox. We watched Becky walk up the front steps and go inside.

Ashley looked at me. "Now what?"

"Follow me!" I said. We circled around to the backyard.

There was a deck with sliding glass doors. Beside that were two windows with a clump of bushes underneath.

I led Ashley behind the bushes. I dropped my backpack to the ground. "Give me a boost so I can look in the window."

"Okay. Be careful." Ashley laced her fingers into a step. I put my foot in and shoved upward to peek in the window. I was looking into a sunny, cheerful kitchen.

"There's Becky!" I whispered excitedly.

"What's she doing?" Ashley whispered back.

"Making microwave popcorn!" I said.

"That's not a clue," Ashley said. "Ow! You're crushing my fingers, Mary-Kate. I hope she does something suspicious fast. I can't hold you up much longer!"

Suddenly we heard a teenage boy's voice from the side yard. "I finished raking the yard, Mom," he called.

Uh-oh. That must be Becky's brother! And it sounded as if he was coming around toward the backyard!

"We'd better hide," Ashley whispered.

I jumped down. We looked around frantically as we grabbed our packs.

A gravel sidewalk led to a small yellow building at the back of the yard.

"The shed!" I said. We dashed for the little building and quickly ducked inside. It was dark and musty-smelling. A small window on one side let in a little sunlight.

We hid behind a lawn mower and some giant bags of potting soil.

"It smells weird in here," I said.

"Shh!" Ashley whispered. "There are footsteps coming this way!"

She slipped her hand into mine. I didn't know whose was trembling the most—mine or hers! What would happen if we got caught in here? We'd be in major trouble!

Then—oh, no! The door creaked open! I peeked out between two bags of potting soil. I could see a blond-haired boy holding a rake.

Ashley and I held our breath.

Would he see us?

He tossed the rake into a corner of the shed. Then—

Slam! Whew! He closed the door.

I let out a big breath. I turned to Ashley. "We're—"

Click!

Uh-oh. "What was that?" I asked.

Ashley's eyes were wide. "It sounded like a lock clicking shut."

We waited a few seconds. Then Ashley tried the door. She rattled it hard.

It didn't open.

My heart sank right down to my toes.

Becky's brother had locked the shed— with us inside!

A Sparkling Clue

"**D**on't worry, Ashley," I said. "There's got to be a way out of here."

We searched the shed. It was too small to have another door.

"The window!" Ashley said.

She tried to open it, but the window wouldn't budge. "I think it's painted shut," she said. "But even if we could open it, it's too small to squeeze through."

I sat down on a paint bucket. "Come on, Ashley. Let's put our heads together. I know we can think of something."

We thought and thought. But there was only one way out. Only one way to keep from spending the whole night in the shed.

Ashley sighed. "We have to yell for help."

"But how will we explain what we were doing in here?" I moaned.

Ashley shrugged. "What else can we do? Who knows when someone will unlock this door again? We could starve in here!"

"Okay, okay," I muttered. "We'll yell. On three, all right? One, two—"

CLICK! CLICK! Someone outside was fumbling with the lock.

We dove back into our hiding place. I peeked out between the two bags.

The blond boy stepped back into the shed. He was grumbling to himself. "Mom always makes me do it again," he muttered. He grabbed the rake. "Who cares if I missed a few spots?"

He grabbed the rake, then left the shed.

The door banged shut.

But he didn't lock it!

"Come on," I whispered. "It's now or never!"

Together we slipped out the door and ran around to the back of the shed.

We made it!

"Come on, Mary-Kate." Ashley tugged on my sleeve. "Let's go home."

I didn't argue. I ran home so fast, Ashley could barely keep up.

The next day Ashley and I spent our entire lunch period trying to find anyone who saw Becky going into or coming out of the gym the day our jerseys disappeared. But no one remembered seeing her.

At the end of the day, we headed to the locker room to change for practice. A few of the other girls came in about the same time.

"This is so frustrating!" Ashley said. "We

know Becky and Jillian are the ones who took the jerseys and messed up the sign. There's got to be a way to prove it!" She glanced at me. "Any new ideas?"

I tugged at my locker door. "I'm stuck."

Ashley shook her head. "Me, too."

"No, I mean I'm really stuck!" I yanked on my locker. "My locker door won't open."

Ashley came over. "Let me try." She pulled and yanked, but it wouldn't open. "Did you spill soda in your locker again?"

"No!" I said.

Kerry gasped. "Hey, my locker's stuck, too!" She banged on it and yanked on it. But it was stuck tight.

"Everyone, check your lockers!" I said.

A few of the lockers opened easily. But Tara and Shanaya discovered that their lockers were stuck, too.

"I don't get it," Kristen said. "It's like they're glued shut."

Glued? I looked closely at my locker.

Tiny purple sparkles glittered around the edge of the opening. I scratched at one little spot.

"That's it!" I said. "They *are* glued. Glitter glued!"

"First, our jerseys disappear. Now this. Maybe our team is jinxed!" Emily said in a scared voice.

"Don't be silly, Emily," Ashley said. "A jinx didn't put glue on our lockers. A person did! Somebody is just playing tricks on us. They're trying to scare us so we'll play badly."

"Becky!" I whispered to Ashley.

Coach Kay got the janitor, Mr. Rivera, to open up our lockers. He pried them open with a screwdriver. "First time I ever saw something like that," he said, scratching his head.

Coach Kay looked worried. But all she said was, "Come on, now, girls. Let's get changed and hit the courts."

We changed as fast as we could. By the time we started, we were a half hour late.

We warmed up by practicing layups. I watched as Tara sank basket after basket.

"She's so good," I said to Ashley. "We really have a great team."

"I know," Ashley agreed. "Tomorrow is the big game. We have to prove that Becky took our jerseys and glued our lockers shut before then. Otherwise she and Jillian may try something else to mess us up."

"Right," I said. "Well, we've got all day tomorrow at school to find the truth. And we're going to do it!"

The next day Ashley and I spent the whole day at school asking everyone if they had seen Becky anywhere near the locker room. Someone must have seen her gluing our lockers shut!

But no one remembered seeing her. "Why would she go near the lockers?" Tim asked. "Our class didn't have gym yesterday."

"How did she do it?" I asked Ashley.

Ashley shook her head. "I don't have a clue. She's really, really sneaky!"

At last the bell rang for the end of school. I jumped up and ran to my cubby to get my stuff.

And then I heard Shanaya shriek in horror!

8

THE CASE FALLS APART

I ran to Shanaya's side. "What's wrong?"

Shanaya held out a piece of paper to me.

"What's this?" I asked.

"A note," she said. Her eyes were wide. "Someone must have stuck it in my cubby when I wasn't looking."

I held up the note as Ashley looked over my shoulder. The note said:

> SIT OUT GAME THREE
> OR YOU'LL BE SORRY!

I handed Shanaya the note, then checked my own cubby. A piece of paper stuck out. I grabbed it and read it. "It's the same note!" I exclaimed.

Ashley had one, too. And so did Kerry.

Ashley and I laid out all the notes and looked at them. They were all written on plain notebook paper with a black marker. All the words were written in capital letters.

"No clues there," I told Ashley.

Shanaya and Kerry looked pretty upset.

"That's it!" I said, upset, too. "We've got to talk to Becky again."

Ashley nodded. "You're right. Come on."

Together we hurried down the hall to Becky's classroom. Tim was just coming out. He was already tearing into a candy bar for his afternoon snack.

"Tim!" I called. "Have you seen Becky?"

Tim started to speak, but his mouth was full of sticky candy. He swallowed at last. "Sorry," he said. "She's not here."

"Where is she?" I asked.

Tim shrugged. "She's out sick today."

"Huh?" I stared at Ashley.

What was going on? How could Becky leave those notes if she wasn't even in school today?

I thought about it some more. If Becky *didn't* leave the notes, then she probably wasn't behind the other pranks, either.

I sucked in my breath. "Ashley, you know what this means, don't you?" I asked.

Ashley nodded. "It means we've been on the wrong trail all along!"

Ashley and I headed home in silence. We had a lot of thinking to do.

Our game wouldn't start till six o'clock. We were supposed to go home and rest.

But I couldn't rest. Not until we solved the case.

As soon as we got home, we ate an early dinner so we'd have plenty of energy for the game. After we finished, we went up to our room. I sat on my bed.

Ashley opened her notebook and stared at her notes about Becky. "What are we missing here?" She put a great big question mark at the top of the page. Then she tossed her notebook aside and flopped back on her bed.

I checked our E-mail.

"Great," I said, reading the computer screen. "The latest edition of *Chatty Patty*."

"Read it to me," Ashley said with a deep sigh.

So I read her the story:

SPORTS NEWS:

MUSTANG GIRLS—ABOUT TO DROP THE BALL?

BY MISS PATTY O'LEARY

CHATTY PATTY SPORTS REPORTER

The Mustang girls' basketball team

is having lots of trouble. Someone has been playing pranks on them. I heard a rumor that two kid detectives are on the case. But they're running out of time. The big game is tonight and they haven't cracked the case!

First, the Mustangs' jerseys disappeared. Then their lockers got glued shut. Today, three of their players got notes warning them not to play in the game.

What's going to happen if they do?

Show up for the game and find out!

"Four," Ashley said.

I looked at her, confused. "What?"

"Four," she repeated. "Patty got it wrong. Four of our players got those notes—not three."

I nodded. "You're right." I got up and began to pace in front of the bed.

Ashley sat up and opened her notebook

again. "Let's write down everything that's happened," she said. "Maybe we'll see something we didn't notice before."

I sighed. "Okay." I sat beside her on the bed.

She wrote down: JERSEYS DISAPPEARED.

"Write down how many," I said. "It might be important."

"Good idea, Mary-Kate," Ashley said. She wrote down the number 4. Her list looked like this:

- 4 JERSEYS DISAPPEARED.
- 1 SCHOOL-SPIRIT SIGN GOT MESSED UP.
- 4 LOCKERS GOT GLUED SHUT.
- 4 PLAYERS GOT THREATENING NOTES.

We stared at the list.

We thought for a minute.

Then we stared at each other. Ashley's eyes lit up.

"Four," we said at the same time.

"Every time something bad happened, it happened to *four* players!" I exclaimed. "Except for the school sign."

"But what could it mean?" Ashley said. "Why are these things happening to just four players?"

"Is it the same four players?" I wondered. "Maybe somebody is mad at those four girls."

Ashley wrote down the names so we could see if there was a pattern.

- 4 JERSEYS DISAPPEARED: ASHLEY, MARY-KATE, TARA, KERRY.
- 4 LOCKERS GOT GLUED SHUT: MARY-KATE, KERRY, TARA, SHANAYA.
- 4 PLAYERS GOT THREATENING NOTES: ASHLEY, MARY-KATE, SHANAYA, KERRY.

"Nope. That's not it." Ashley sighed. She crumpled up the list and put it on the bed.

"Don't worry, we'll figure it out," I said. I

took Ashley's crumpled-up paper ball and shot it toward the trash can in the corner.

Plonk! It went in!

"Two points!" I exclaimed. Then I slumped on the bed. Too bad I didn't shoot like that in the last game.

"Why would four be important to our team?" Ashley wondered, reading over our list. "What good would it do for four players not to play? How could that help Jillian and her team? I don't get it."

I shrugged. "It's not even like they tried to get the top four players not to play. Tara's our top player. And she didn't get a note warning her not to play."

We thought some more. Four, four, four. What could it mean?

I borrowed Ashley's notebook.

"We have nine players on our team." I wrote down the number 9. "And five girls get to play at one time." I wrote down 5.

We stared at the numbers.

9 PLAYERS

5 PLAYERS ON THE COURT

No fours there.
Suddenly Ashley gasped.
"I've got it!" she cried.

9

THE SUBTRACTION SOLUTION

"**W**hat?" I cried. "Tell me, Ashley!"

"I see the pattern," Ashley said. She wrinkled her forehead. "I'm just not sure what it means."

"Girls! Time to go!" our mom called up the stairs. "Better hurry—we're running a little late."

"Come on," Ashley said. She stood up. "I'll explain on the way back to school. And then we can try to figure out what it all means."

"Before game time," I added, gulping.

We had to work fast!

We climbed into the car to head back to school. Ashley and I sat in the backseat with our heads bent over her notebook.

"Here's what I saw," she told me. She showed me where she had written down "9 players" and "5 players on the court." She wrote a minus sign next to the five. "Finish the math problem," she said.

So I did a little subtraction problem on her notepad.

$$\begin{array}{r} 9 \text{ PLAYERS} \\ -5 \text{ PLAYERS ON THE COURT} \\ \hline 4 \text{ PLAYERS ON THE BENCH} \end{array}$$

My eyes popped open wide. "Hey! There's our four!"

"Right. What would happen if four of our starting players didn't play in the game?" Ashley asked.

"Then all four girls on the bench would definitely get to play!" I exclaimed. I frowned. "That wouldn't help the Tigers."

"But it *would* help the girls on the bench," Ashley said.

I looked at Ashley. I didn't want to say it out loud.

Ashley sighed. "I hate to even think this, but...somebody on our own team has been doing these mean things."

"The question is—who?" I asked.

We stared at each other. I was starting to get an idea. I thought I knew who was behind all the pranks!

But before I could say anything, our mom pulled into a parking space. "Here we are," she said. "Mary-Kate, Ashley, isn't that your coach by the door, waving at you? You'd better go on in."

Coach Kay looked worried. Ashley and I climbed out of the car and hurried toward her. "Have a good game, girls," Mom called.

"Have you girls heard from Tara?" Coach Kay asked as we ran up to her.

"No, why?" I asked.

Coach Kay shook her head. "She's usually the first one here, but she hasn't shown up yet, and the game starts in fifteen minutes." She gave us a small smile. "It's probably nothing, though. Let's get inside."

"I'm sure Tara will be here any second," Ashley said as we walked inside. "This game is super important to her."

Then, as I walked past Tara's locker, I spotted something. A crumpled piece of paper on the floor.

I picked it up and smoothed it out. Then I read it—and gasped. "Oh, no! Listen to this! 'Tara—The game has been postponed two hours. It won't start till eight.'"

Everyone on the team gasped. The game would be over by then!

"And it's signed…" I looked at my sister. "Ashley."

10

THE BIG GAME

"**M**e?" Ashley exclaimed. "I didn't write that note!"

"We know you wouldn't do something like that," Samantha said.

"What's important right now is to get Tara back here for the game," Coach Kay said. "I'll try calling her house."

The coach stepped into her office, which was right off the locker room. We all watched her dial. I knew what we were all thinking: *Tara is our best player. She can't*

miss the big game! She can't!

Coach Kay put down the phone. "The line's busy," she said. She checked her watch. "We still have ten minutes. I'll keep trying."

"Ashley," I whispered. "Do you still have the note you got in your cubby this afternoon?"

"I stuck it in my notebook," Ashley said. She pulled it out. We compared it to Tara's note.

"The handwriting is the same," I said. "I think I know who wrote these notes."

"Who?" Ashley asked.

"The one girl on the bench who's not always so nice," I said. "The one who complains about the coach. And about not getting to play. The one who says mean things when other players make mistakes." I drew in a deep breath. "I think it's Emily Bailey."

Ashley's eyes widened. Then she nodded. "You're right—it has to be Emily. And we have to talk to her—now."

Most of the other players were crowded around Coach Kay's desk. But Emily stood by her locker, gathering her curly hair into a ponytail. Ashley and I went over to her.

"It was you, wasn't it, Emily?" I asked in a quiet voice. "You wrote that note to Tara."

Emily's freckled cheeks turned a little pale. "What?"

"And you're the one who pulled all the other pranks, too. Hiding the jerseys, and gluing the lockers shut, and sending everyone those mean notes," Ashley added. "Right?"

Emily's eyes opened wide. "No way!" she cried.

"Come on, Emily," I said. "You're always complaining about never getting a chance to play."

"And you had an easy way to get your hands on the team jerseys," Ashley added. "Your dad's laundry service cleans them."

"And what about the glitter glue on the lockers?" I said. "You're in our art class. You could have easily taken the glitter glue we used on our window hangings."

"*And* you're in our class. It would have been simple for you to slip those mean notes into our cubbies," Ashley said.

Emily's face turned bright red. "It isn't true. You can't prove it!" she cried.

"Yes, we can," I said quietly. I reached into her open locker and pulled out a tiny tube of sparkly purple glue. "Here's the proof. The glitter glue you used to glue our lockers shut."

Emily's eyes suddenly filled with tears. She sank down on the bench. "Okay, I admit it. I did it."

Ashley sat down beside her. "Why?" she asked.

"I was dying for a chance to play in a real play-off game," Emily said. "My dad keeps bragging to everyone that I'm on the team—but Coach hardly ever lets me play!"

She buried her face in her hands.

Ashley and I looked at each other. We were glad to solve the case. But seeing Emily cry made us feel awful.

"You must really love basketball," I said.

Emily sniffed. "Mmm-hmmm. My dad and I watch it on TV all the time." She wiped the tears from her eyes. "I'm sorry," she said. "I know I really messed up. I wish I could take it all back." She was silent for a minute. "I guess you'll have to tell Coach Kay, huh."

"I don't know," I said. "Tricking Tara was a pretty bad thing to do."

I glanced at the coach's office. Coach Kay hung up the phone, shaking her head.

"Tara's line must still be busy," Ashley said.

"Hey!" Emily jumped to her feet. "I know. Tara doesn't live very far away. I'll get my dad to drive to her house and pick her up! At least I can fix one of the bad things I did."

I smiled. "Great idea!"

Emily ran into the gym to find her dad.

At the same time I saw the Tigers run out onto the court to warm up. The game was about to begin.

I looked around at our teammates' faces. Everyone seemed nervous—but ready. We headed on to the court.

The whistle blew, and the game began. We played pretty well—for a team whose star player was missing! But the Tigers played better. Soon they were eight points ahead.

I kept watching the door. Where were Emily and Tara? Would they show up in time to play?

I caught sight of Princess Patty sitting in the very front row of the bleachers. She was scribbling away in her reporter's notebook.

I swallowed hard and turned my mind back to the game.

The first quarter ended. Then the second. It was halftime. The Tigers were ten points ahead. Still no Emily. No Tara.

As I stood by the bench, I glanced up in the stands—and spotted Becky. She was sitting with Tim—and they were holding up a sign that said MUSTANGS RULE!

I pointed it out to Ashley. "We sure were wrong about her," I said.

Ashley nodded. "She couldn't help that she used to be friends with Jillian. I guess she really was trying to stop Jillian from messing up our sign."

"Let's go apologize to her," I said.

Ashley and made our way up to where Becky was sitting. She looked at us and scowled. "What do you want?" she asked.

"We're here to apologize," Ashley said.

"Yeah," I added. "We're really sorry we accused you of messing with our team. We know now that you didn't do it."

"We shouldn't have jumped to conclusions," Ashley said.

Becky hesitated. Then she said, "It's okay, I guess. I was pretty upset when you accused me of all those things. But I know you were just worried about your team. You must like basketball as much as I do."

"If you like basketball so much, you should try out for the Mustangs next year," Ashley suggested. "We would love it if you were our teammate."

A smile lit Becky's face. "I'd like that a lot!" she said.

"Look!" we heard Samantha shout from below. "Tara's here!"

I spun around. Tara was hurrying up the sidelines. Right behind her was Emily! She gave Ashley and me a thumbs-up.

"All right!" Ashley, Becky, and I cheered. We all slapped high fives.

"It's time to show those Tigers a thing or

two about basketball!" I shouted. Ashley and I headed back to the bench.

"Emily explained everything," Tara told Ashley and me in a low voice, once we reached the sidelines.

"And you're not mad?" I asked.

"Yes, I am," Tara said. "But...well, I love basketball more than anything in the world, too. So I understand why she did it."

Before Tara could say anything more, Coach Kay rushed over with her jersey. Then the whistle blew for the second half, and Tara stormed onto the court.

It was just the boost we needed. In the second half of the game, the Mustangs caught fire! By the end of the third quarter, we were only three points down.

In the fourth quarter, no one seemed able to score. The Mustangs blocked all the Tigers' shots. The Tigers blocked all the Mustangs' shots.

With three minutes left, Shanaya made a

basket. Now we were just one point behind. But Shanaya fell and hurt her knee.

Coach Kay pulled Shanaya out—and sent Emily in!

Emily beamed as she ran onto the court.

Ashley had the ball. She dribbled down the court. But then the Tigers surrounded her. She looked for someone to pass to.

Emily was open. Ashley passed it to her.

With seconds to go, Emily charged down the court.

She had a chance to shoot. But there were four Tigers between her and the basket.

I was right under the basket. "Emily!" I shouted. I waved to her, showing her I was open.

Emily hesitated.

I knew what she was thinking. This was her big chance. Her big chance to make a basket and prove she was a good player.

But I was in a better spot to shoot. And we had to make this basket to win the game!

What would Emily do?

I watched as she raised her arms to shoot. Then she gave a big grin—and bounced the ball over to me!

I was so surprised, I almost didn't catch it. But I did. I dribbled once—and leaped toward the basket.

Time seemed to slow down as the ball left my fingers. It sailed toward the hoop.

And then—*SWISH!*

The ball sank through the net. Two points!

A second later the referee's whistle blew. Game over!

I glanced around as the gym burst into cheers. This time the cheers were coming from our side.

We won! We were on our way to the championship!

Let Princess Patty write about that!

Our teammates bunched together in the middle of the court. We were laughing and hugging. Ashley and I threw our arms around each other. Then we threw our arms around Emily.

"Thanks," Emily said, grinning at us both.

Ashley and I slapped a high five.

Teamwork won the game—and solved the crime!

Hi from both of us,

Ashley and I were picked to be part of the Sparkles—a rock band! We had been practicing for months. Now our first concert was only a few days away.

But someone wasn't as excited for our concert as we were. Our singer's hair was ruined when someone switched his shampoo with hair dye. And all our instruments were stolen from right under our noses! If we didn't find out who was trying to stop the music, our concert would be ruined. Who didn't want the show to go on? That's what we had to figure out—fast!

Do you want to find out more? Take a look at the next page for a sneak peek at The New Adventures of Mary-Kate & Ashley: *The Case of the Rock Star's Secret*.

See you next time!

Mary-Kate
Olsen

Ashley
Olsen

The Case Of The
ROCK STAR'S SECRET

The next morning Ashley and I rode our bikes to rehearsal at the Sparkle mansion. "I can't believe it," I said. "Only one more day until the big concert. One more day until Johnny Sparkle's incredible mansion becomes our town's new music center!"

We pulled into the driveway of the mansion. Ashley led the way inside. We hurried down the long hallway and through the double doors leading to the concert hall.

Andrew Baxter, our lead singer, stood on the stage. His red hair was gleaming in the stage lights.

"Hey, Andrew!" I called. Ashley and I climbed up the steps to join him.

Larry McHugh, our band assistant, came out from the wings. He stood next to Andrew and patted his own red hair. "Two redheads are better than one, right? I think maybe I should do a duet with Andrew," he suggested.

I glanced at Ashley. She rolled her eyes. Larry was always trying to get into the act. The problem was, he couldn't sing at all.

"I don't think we should add anything to the act the day before the concert," our keyboard player, Johnny Krause, called. He trotted down the left aisle and swung himself up onto the stage.

"I'm just trying to make the show the best it can be," Larry muttered. He checked his clipboard. "I noticed you guys are almost out of cherry soda. Can anyone think of anything else we need before tomorrow night?"

Johnny shook his head. "You always think of everything before the rest of us even have a chance to," he said.

"It's true," I jumped in. "You're a great assistant."

"Maybe you'll be a real band manager, like Sunshine Boyd, someday!" Ashley added.

"I guess that might be cool," Larry said. But he didn't sound too happy. "I'll be back in about twenty minutes. I expect to hear some rehearsing when I get back."

He started off the stage, then turned around. "Oh, I almost forgot. Sunshine dropped these off before you guys got here." Larry handed each of us a bright yellow button with a sun drawn on it. "He said they're for good luck tomorrow," he added.

"That's so sweet!" Ashley exclaimed.

"He didn't give me one. I guess assistants don't need good luck," Larry grumbled as he stomped off stage.

"Let's get started," Johnny said.

I strapped on the black and red guitar I'd

picked out from Johnny Sparkle's collection. Ashley positioned herself behind the drum set. Johnny sat down at the keyboard. Andrew strapped on his bass guitar and moved up to the mike at the front of the stage.

"Let's start with *Happy Birthday*," Johnny suggested.

Ashley counted it off on her drumsticks. "One, and two, and three, and—"

We launched into the song. We planned to play it at the very end of the concert. We figured it would give everyone in the audience time to think about Johnny Sparkle. And we hoped that somehow, some way, Johnny would be able to hear it, too.

We rehearsed *Happy Birthday* three times. Then Johnny asked, "Want to move on to *Alligator Tango* now?"

"I could use a little more work on that one," Ashley agreed. "One, and two, and—"

KA-BOOM!

KA-BOOM! KA-BOOM! KA-BOOM!

"What's that?" I yelled.

"Something's exploding!" Andrew yelled back. "It sounds like it's coming from the backyard!"

I jerked off the guitar and set it on the stage. Then I leaped down to the concert hall floor and flew toward the double doors. Ashley was right behind me.

"Be careful, Mary-Kate!" she cried.

I kept running. Out the double doors. Down the long hallway. Through the stained-glass doors.

And we were outside. The first thing I saw was a small, scorched spot on the cement by the pool. A few scraps of red paper were scattered on top of it.

Ashley picked one of the scraps up and studied it. "Cherry bomb," she announced.

"Hey, Ashley! Mr. and Mrs. Zane—those people who live down the street—said some kids in the neighborhood have been setting off cherry bombs," I said. "Remember?"

Ashley nodded. "That must be it."

We all headed back inside. We ran into Larry as we reached the concert hall door. He was flushed and breathing hard. His red hair was glued to his forehead with sweat.

"What's going on? Why aren't you guys practicing?" he asked breathlessly.

"We heard this explosion outside and we went to check it out," Andrew explained. "Some kids set off cherry bombs."

I led the way back into the concert hall. I glanced toward the stage. "Hey, Larry, I don't want to tell you how to do your job—but shouldn't you wait to clean the instruments until *after* rehearsal?" I asked.

"What are you talking about?" Larry demanded.

My stomach turned over.

"You took the instruments backstage to clean them, didn't you?" I asked.

"No. I just got back with the soda," Larry said. He held up the plastic bag in his hand. "It's right here."

My stomach turned over again.

"Well *someone* did something with them," I cried. I pointed at the stage—the *empty* stage. "Because they're gone!"

Take a Peek Inside our Diaries!

T'S YOUR FIRST CLASS
ICKET TO ADVENTURE!

Mary-Kate Ashley

Take a peek at the new Fashion Dolls!

Coming your way Spring 2000!

DUALSTAR
ENTERTAINMENT
GROUP

www.marykateandashley.com   www.barbie.com

Each sold separately.

© 1999 Mattel, Inc. All Rights Reserved.
TM & © 1999 Dualstar Entertainment Group, Inc. All Rights Reserved.

GAME GIRLS

MARY-KATE & ASHLEY

SOLVE ANY CRIME BY DINNER TIME™

The New Adventures of
MARY-KATE & ASHLEY™

GAME BOY COLOR

PARTY DOWN WITH THE HOTTEST DANCES AND COOLEST FASHIONS

MARY-KATE & ASHLEY's DANCE PARTY of the CENTURY™

PC CD-ROM

www.marykateandashley.com

DUALSTAR INTERACTIVE

www.acclaim.net

It doesn't matter if you live around the corner...
or around the world...
If you are a fan of Mary-Kate & Ashley Olsen,
you should be a member of

Mary-Kate + Ashley's Fun Club™

Here's what you get
Our Funzine™
An autographed color photo
Two black & white individual photos
A full-sized color poster
An official Fun Club™ school folder
Two special Fun Club™ surprises
Fun Club™ Collectibles Catalog
Plus a Fun Club™ box to keep everything in.

To join Mary-Kate + Ashley's Fun CLub™,
fill out the form below and send it, along with
U.S. Residents $17.00
Canadian Residents $22.00 (US Funds only)
International Residents $27.00 (US Funds only)

Mary-Kate + Ashley's Fun CLub™
859 Hollywood Way PMB 275
Burbank, CA 91505

Name:_____

Address:_____

City:_____ St:_____ Zip:_____

Phone: (_____) _____

E-Mail: _____

or fax your credit card order to us at (818) 785-2275

Card Number:_____ Exp: _____

Cardholders Name: _____

Cardholders Signature: _____

Attn. Canadian and International Residents
We are no longer accepting personal checks drawn on non U.S. banks.
For ease of ordering, we recommend payment via credit card
(Visa or Mastercard only please)
Check us out on the web at
www.marykateandashley.com